Lyres, Legends, and Lullabies
AN ANNOTATED SCORE COLLECTION

By Author & Composer
R. L. Davennor

Printed in the United States of America

First Printing, 2020

ISBN 978-1-7351315-0-4

Published by Night Muse Press
https://www.nightmusepress.com

Cover art by Hannah Sternjakob Design
https://www.hannah-sternjakob-design.com/

Paperback formatting by The Illustrated Author Design Services
https://www.theillustratedauthor.net/

To Jesse, my light in the dark.
Thank you for being my everything.

ACKNOWLEDGMENTS

Jesse may be my everything, but Jena, you're my everything else! I would be lost without you.
To Kaitlin, Katie, Zoltán, and Marie, my dear friends. Without your endless encouragement and kind words, this creation would not exist.
To everyone who's ever had a dream: If I can do it, so can you. In case no one's ever told you, I believe in you.
Go out there and kick some ass.

CONTENTS

PREFACE

I never intended to be a composer.

For many years, I *refused* to refer to myself as such. The title felt so formal, so unattainable, and so alien that I never entertained the idea. Melodies of my own creation swirled through my mind from the start of my musical education, but that made perfect sense: I was a musician, like so many of my friends and colleagues, and surely, they heard them too. A musician was nothing special. A composer—a *creator*—was the rarest of them all.

I've *always* wanted to be an author.

For as long as music has filled my mind, so have stories. Dragons, demons, castles, royalty, magic, and distant shores have never failed to whisk me away to far-off lands that were always superior to my own. While I love reading and continue to consume as many books as I can get my hands on, the stories they told were never enough.

I needed to write my own.

But for so long, life got in the way. I chose to pursue music as a career, and at some point, convinced myself it was impossible to write a book, finish my studies, support myself financially, *and* come out sane. Though there was probably some truth to that sentiment, in many ways, fear was my real ball and chain. Fear of not being good enough, of being undeserving of any good that might come my way, and of course, the fear of rejection and failure. I was forced to face each of them and more before I ever saw light at the end of my tunnel. I was told during my initial audition that I wasn't skilled enough to be accepted. I had a composition mocked in front of my classmates. I was scolded by conductors in front of an entire orchestra. In my darkest hour, I was urged to consider changing my major by a teacher I deeply respected.

I cried. I quivered with anger and rage. I spent most nights alone, a slave to my reed desk, studying and practicing until I was so exhausted, I could no longer see straight. But above all...I listened to the music that had been there all along.

I won auditions and chair placements. I earned every ounce of respect my teachers gave to me by my final year of study. I performed and passed a master's recital. I graduated with honors and made history by being a member of the first wind quintet invited to perform at the commencement ceremony.

I became the heroine of my own tale, slaying monsters and breaking chains, and it was high time I wrote one.

Lyres, Legends, and Lullabies is everything I thought I would never be, but always dreamed I could become. While not every score has a story, each is a part of mine. You will gain unprecedented insight into how each of these pieces came to be and experience the music alongside prose and my own annotations. This book is for anyone with a dream—musician or not—and proof that no matter how treacherous your path, you *can* survive.

Listen along as you read!
https://soundcloud.com/rldavennor/sets/lyres-legends-and-lullabies

RISE

Scored for Solo Piano

Composed March 2020

With my own skill at the keyboard limited at best, it's always a challenge to make sure anything I compose is not only playable but as full-sounding to my ear as it's used to hearing in larger ensembles. I'm fond of lots of pedal, a repetitive bassline, and utilizing the full range of the instrument wherever possible.

Arise began with the melody stated by the right hand, and the bass line was discovered very much by accident. As I continued to develop the theme, the slow, yet deliberate buildup reminded me of my character Alexandria Somara. Outwardly, she is calm, meek, and collected, but prod her inner fire, and she will always rise to the challenge.

In my written works, *Arise* as a title appears twice: once as the title of the novella where Alex is the main character and a second time as one of *Bloodlust's* chapters. The word now forever holds ties to her, just as this piece became her anthem.

Listen here:
https://soundcloud.com/rldavennor/arise

Excerpt from *Bloodlust*, Chapter XIII. Arise

The Elder said nothing for a long while. Eventually, he narrowed his gaze and emitted a low rumble. "*So there remains the Eldest...and you.*"

You—spat like the insult Alex knew it was. She'd tolerated being struck. She'd allowed them to speak of her as if she weren't right in front of them.

But she would *not* stand for this.

Alex spoke before Aymrie could stop her. "*Luke is a traitor undeserving of such a title. I am Eldest now.*"

Nulmirn growled. "*You're—*"

"*Too young? Too inexperienced? Too useless?*" Alex snapped. "*I have studied for seven years and proven myself in every way imaginable. I will be senior and mentor to Kia and Elizabeth's heirs—the very definition of Eldest. It is your problem if I am still not enough.*"

With her shout still echoing off the walls surrounding them, Alex turned and walked away. Aymrie followed close at her heels, struggling to match Alex's hurried pace as behind them, the council broke into yet another argument. She gritted her teeth. The sooner they were out of here, the better.

Are you certain that was a good idea?

It was a horrible idea, but it sure felt good. For once, Alex found herself eager to face the Falls—the frigid water might soothe some of the swelling on her face.

Realizing her intention, Aymrie slowed. *We're leaving so soon?*

I'd rather sleep in a ditch than spend another second in that asshole's presence.

Aymrie rumbled, darting ahead to take the lead. *In that case, I'll find us a comfortable ditch.*

Though her cheeks ached, Alex smiled.

ARISE

R. L. DAVENNOR

The Arrival

Scored for:

Whistle in D	*Guitar*
Low Whistle in D	*Bouzouki*
Gemshorn	*2 Bodhrans*
Uilleann Pipes	*Bumbac*
Fiddle	*Kettle Drum*
Harp	*Bass Drum*

Composed February 2020

This piece was originally intended to be Alex's 'theme,' and although it remains heavily influenced by her motifs, it deviated into something else. The opening melody borrows from *Alexandria's Awakening*, and the middle section features melodies directly quoted from one of my earliest pieces: *Sage's Hymn*. Eb minor is the key center I associate with Alexandria. It is grounded, natural, and of the earth, all traits Alex possesses.

The Arrival guides the listener through the Enchanters' arrival at the Dragon Temple. For Rebecca and Tristan, it is their first time visiting the ancient structure, and the Sages offer them a warm, musical welcome.

Listen here:

https://soundcloud.com/rldavennor/the-arrival

Excerpt from *Bloodlust*, Chapter XVI. Pact

Alex beamed as she faced front. "We've arrived."

Aymrie picked up her pace without prompting just as the faint beating of drums began. Each strike mirrored the pounding of Alex's heart as they raced through the remaining overgrowth, the music growing stronger and more powerful with each step her dragon took. Alex heard Rebecca and Tristan calling for her, but she didn't slow. She wanted to see their faces when they took in the Dragon Temple for the first time—and one quite a bit more than the other.

A flute began to sing a familiar melody the moment firelight pierced through the blackness. Alex urged Aymrie even faster when she heard voices, heart swelling at the thought of seeing Darius and Bianca again so soon.

My, you're excited.

It's the little things.

Parted gates and a horde of Sages awaited them. Dozens of carefully-placed torches illuminated the latticework of vines, and although the Sages' inner circle, including Titus, stood front and center, Darius was nowhere to be found. Alex's eyes narrowed as she dismounted Aymrie. Where *was* he?

Tristan arrived next, mouth agape as the Sages wearing silver robes surrounded his dragon. It proved to be a bit too soon for the glacidrákon; he reared up, wings beating and limbs flailing until Tristan could calm him. The music continued despite his fear, with the increasing tempo and volume of the pipes stirring something within Alex's soul.

Titus knelt as Tristan dismounted, and the others followed suit. Alex rolled her eyes as Titus introduced himself to Tristan with far more sincerity than he'd ever offered her.

Tristan gave his name when prompted before turning to his dragon. "This is Rogun."

Rogun. Alex mouthed the name silently; she hadn't thought to ask the glacidrákon's name before, but neither had Tristan asked about Aymrie. Alex huffed, turning away to scan the trees for Rebecca as the crowd continued to converse.

There. Though the okedrákon Sages stepped forward to welcome their Enchantress, Alex shoved past them all, heart swelling when Sitora emerged from the forest. She alone had the major advantage of knowing what to expect, but whatever warning she'd given Rebecca hadn't been enough. She gasped audibly as she took in what lay before her, tensing and shrinking back as if the Sages carried weapons meant to harm her.

"It's all right," Alex called, and Rebecca's gaze snapped to her. "Let me help you."

Sitora knelt for Rebecca to dismount just as the music reached its peak. With Alex by her side, Rebecca relaxed, but only slightly. Around them, the sea of Sages parted, and Alex led the way to the gates.

"This is all for us?" Rebecca whispered.

"Every bit of it."

Rebecca's fingers fumbled for Alex's hand. "There are so many of them."

"You needn't be afraid. I understand it's a large crowd—"

"The last time I met a Sage, it went poorly." Rebecca planted her feet in the dust. "Will they truly take our weapons?"

Alex nodded. "But it is safe, I assure you."

"It had better be." Rebecca's eyes flashed as she nodded in the Sages' direction. "They seem to want to speak to me."

"They do. They'll see you to your chambers, and make sure they care for your wound—"

"Talk in the morning?" Rebecca interrupted.

Alex nodded, and Rebecca slipped away. Little by little, the procession began to file into the gates, but Alex hardly noticed when her bow and quiver were taken from her. Still no sign of Darius, so she snatched Titus's shoulder as he brushed past.

"Where is Darius?" she demanded.

"The Head Sage requested not to be disturbed for the remainder of the evening."

Alex's eyes burned—bullshit. If Darius were here, he'd have come to see her. Arms crossed, she watched him stalk away, remaining where she stood as the music died. The celebration was certainly over. When fingers curled around her arm, Alex yanked herself free, much to Helen's surprise.

"Enchantress Alex, it isn't safe to be standing out here—"

"We'll see ourselves to our chambers, thanks."

With Aymrie at her heels, Alex stepped through the gates.

THE ARRIVAL

R. L. DAVENNOR

14

Alexandria's Awakening

Scored for:

2 Flutes	*Tuba*
2 Oboes (1 doubling English Horn)	*Timpani*
2 Clarinets in Bb	*Chimes*
2 Bassoons	*Bass Drum*
4 Horns	*Snare Drum*
2 Trumpets in Bb	*Cymbal*
2 Trombones	*String Orchestra*

Composed February 2019

Alexandria's Awakening was one the first pieces I composed for a full symphony orchestra, and the magnitude of it baffles me to this day. I recall the orchestration coming to me without much struggle, despite being worried about writing the brass parts, and I completed the piece in a little over a week. For reference, subsequent works for full orchestra have sat for weeks, even months on end.

All I can say is that Alex truly inspires me.

The piece is paired with the inciting incident of my novella *Arise*. Having discovered a shocking betrayal and bearing witness to a tragic accident, Alex is faced with an impossible choice: remain where she is and be shipped off to a man she doesn't wish to marry, or flee for her life into the unknown. She chooses the latter, but is pursued into the forest by her father's men. What happens after that changes her life forever, in ways she never could have imagined.

Listen here:
https://soundcloud.com/rldavennor/alexandrias-awakening

Excerpt from *Arise*, Chapter II. The Escape

A dragon.
A dragon.

Heart and mind racing, Alex's feet moved of their own accord, and not back toward her chambers. They led her down the stairs, through the passageways, and to the outside, following a pull she couldn't explain. She shouldn't help. She *couldn't* help, for all she knew.

But she had to try.

The beast was wounded even before it fell, otherwise it would have flown...*right?* It had wings, and presumably knew how to use them. But who would have wounded such a magnificent creature—much less the only dragon anyone had seen for hundreds of years? Though all she saw was stone and blackness, her mind couldn't stop picturing the shape of it. Those gorgeous green scales. Those *eyes.*

The eyes that glowed like hers.

Alex reached the courtyard and raced towards the motionless silhouette. *No.* She gritted her teeth, calling forth her power before she ever reached the creature, allowing the magic to envelop her palms.

No. Don't be gone.

When she knelt by its side, the dragon didn't move.

She didn't have to be a healer to know its body was broken. Its limbs splayed out at grotesque angles. Its wings bent over like fallen banners. Its eyes remained open but lacked their glow.

No.

"You cannot help."

Alex whirled around. Darius stood not far off, face stony and expressionless.

She scoffed. "You haven't even let me try."

He nodded towards the dragon. "Alex, look."

She turned back towards the beast and watched the body crumple into dust.

Alexandria's Awakening

R. L. Davennor

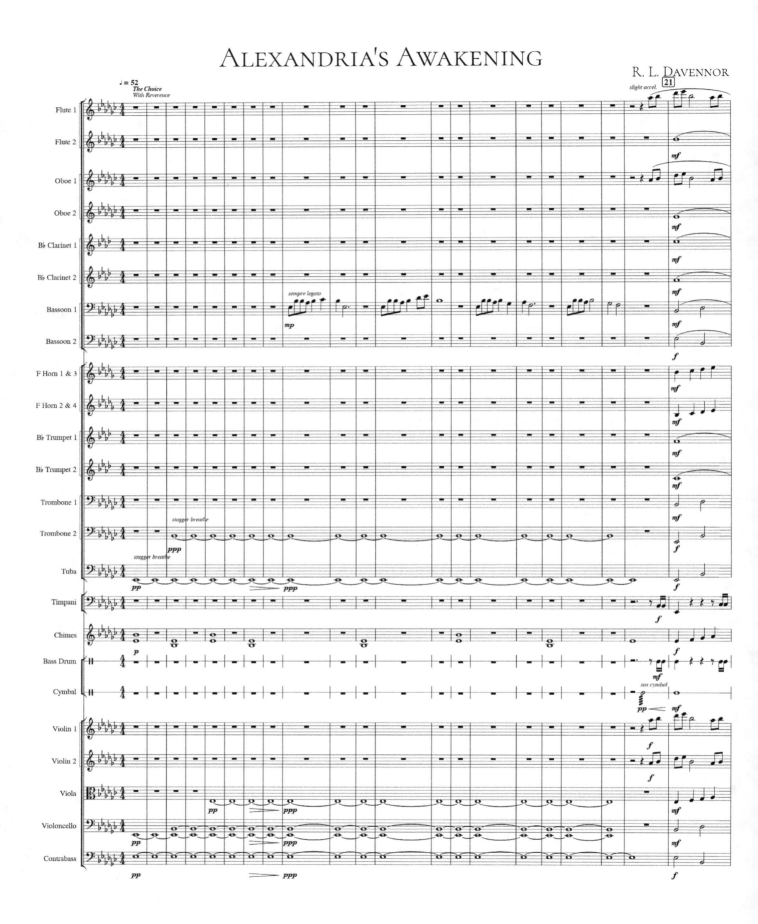

37
Fl. 1
Fl. 2
Ob. 1
Ob. 2
B♭ Cl. 1
B♭ Cl. 2
Bsn. 1
Bsn. 2
F Hn. 1 3
F Hn. 2 4
B♭ Tpt. 1
B♭ Tpt. 2
Tbn. 1
Tbn. 2
Tba.
Timp.
Cme.
B. Dr.
Vln. 1
Vln. 2
Vla.
Vc.
Cb.
f
mf
8

The Beast Within

Scored for:

Whistle in D	*Hurdy Gurdy*
Oboe	*Bodhran*
Uilleann Pipes	*Bumbac*
Fiddle	*Kettle Drum*
Bouzouki	

Composed December 2019

The Beast Within was born out of me wanting to compose a piece for solo Hurdy Gurdy. I'd developed a newfound love and appreciation for the instrument, and I was eager to add to its repertoire, until I got a little carried away with the melody. The original statement in 6/4 gets restated in 6/8, and in quite a livelier, dance-like fashion. I added instruments that fit the dance, and built from there.

In the end, it was really the oboe's haunting statement that convinced me to pair this piece with writing. I immediately thought of Rebecca's wedding, and the moment where her shapeshifting magic manifests itself for the first time. While the crowd surrounding her glimpses who she really is, Rebecca gets her first glimpse of the woman with whom she is inexplicably linked…

Listen here:
https://soundcloud.com/rldavennor/the-beast-within

Excerpt from *Bloodlust*, Chapter IV. Threads

A sudden quiet fell over the room as voices dropped out one by one. The musicians in the far corner had been playing lively tunes all throughout the meal, but seemed to be gearing up for something else. The floor in front of the married couple cleared, leaving ample space for the one tradition Rebecca had forgotten. The dance.

"Fuck," William spat, mirroring Rebecca's thoughts exactly. He stood before she did, moving at a rapid pace despite his intoxication, and dragged Rebecca to the floor. "Let's get this over with."

He wrapped his free arm around her waist and pulled her against his hips. Despite their closeness, a strange part of her trusted him as she realized this was just as important for William as it was for her. The first dance was more than just custom. It was about togetherness, and a public assessment of their strength and future success as a couple. Arms bound, hands crisscrossed, and feet poised to leap, every pair of eyes was on them.

The room fell silent save for Rebecca's pounding heart.

A slight nod of William's head was the only cue the musicians needed. A drone so low it vibrated the floor set the tone while a melody began in an instrument cranked with a wheel. The drummer brought the others in one by one: a whistle, a fiddle, and pipes. This was a completely different tune than the one to which they rehearsed, yet somehow, Rebecca felt as though she'd heard it before. As the song gathered strength and speed at a rapid pace, it awakened a slumbering presence within her. She straightened, standing tall as she met William's gaze.

She knew how to handle herself with a sword. This was simply different choreography.

The tune began, harsh and wild, and Rebecca followed suit. Now that she attributed the steps to her training with Tristan, her feet grazed the ground with practiced ease. She squared her shoulders and raised her arms, eyes blazing with dragonsfire.

William forgot when it came time to clap, shooting Rebecca a glare as she yanked their hands into position. The pace quickened. Rebecca's dress became harder to dodge, and her hair whipped William in the face on more than one occasion. She forgot about the crowd, and despite the restriction of the bonds encircling her wrist, she felt free for the first time since arriving in Ide.

Warmth blossomed in her chest. Rebecca threw back her head, sending raven curls spilling over her shoulders. She could see green reflected on the vaulted stone ceiling, enveloping the entire room with her light. The longer they danced and the faster the drums beat, the more exhilarated she felt. Rebecca whirled and spun, her movements matching the rhythm with ease.

The world around her faded away, and the music stopped save for the drone. A voice called to her, longing and beautiful, and Rebecca came to a halt. Her chest heaved with each breath as the song ceased to make room for words that she'd heard once before.

I am here for you.

The Beast Within

R. L. Davennor

CHASING DESTINY

Scored for:

Celeste	*Bass Drum*
Piano	*Cymbal*

String Orchestra Composed July 2018

Some of my earliest writing was done on online forums. In both small groups and one-on-one pairings, I participated in co-telling a story, and not only was it invaluable learning and practice, I made incredible friends. After a while, I even mustered enough courage to begin composing music for the stories we made together.

This is exactly how *Chasing Destiny* came into being.

There is no excerpt to go with this piece; not because it's been lost, but because it wouldn't make much sense without context, and also because I've sadly lost contact with this particular partner. She created an incredible character named Scarlett (this piece was originally titled *Scarlett's Destiny*) and I composed this piece for an emotional point in the narrative where Scarlett is closer than ever before to accomplishing her goal. The celeste's melody is meant to be a lullaby Scarlett's mother used to sing to her, and the rest of the piece centers around building toward it.

Tessa, if you're reading this, I miss you, and will be forever grateful for the story we wrote together!

Listen here:

https://soundcloud.com/rldavennor/chasing-destiny

CHASING DESTINY

R. L. DAVENNOR

CHOSEN BY THE BLOOD

Scored for:

Voice	*Guitar*
Oboe	*Cello*
Whistle in D	*Double Bass*

Composed December 2019

Chosen by the Blood is another piece intended to be composed for solo guitar, but once again my love for melody won out. I knew nothing of the lyrics other than the singular line "chosen by the blood," and based everything around that syllable pattern. The rest of the instruments were added into my arrangement for effect, and the piece could still be performed by solo guitar and voice.

The lyrics are a lullaby Arakunian mothers sing to their children, warning them of the days infants were being stolen by the dragons for, at that time, unknown reasons. All they knew was that it involved blood magic, and that such magic brought dire consequences.

To be chosen by the blood meant death.

Lyrics:
Rest your eyes or they will come for you
Bite your tongue, they'll take you too
Children lost within the night
Chosen by the blood

Dragons call all through the wind and rain
From the ashes, one remains
Stay too long, hear their song
You will find yourself chosen by the blood

Sleep my child, don't let them see you cry
Destiny can be denied
You are safe within my arms
Child of the blood

Listen here:
https://soundcloud.com/rldavennor/chosen-by-the-blood

CHOSEN BY THE BLOOD

R. L. DAVENNOR

You are safe with-in my arms chi-ld of the blood

ENCHANTRESS

Scored for Solo Piano

Composed March 2020

    Enchantress was composed in one sitting, and originated from the lone melody stated in the beginning. From there, several other motifs presented themselves, and despite my lingering reservations about composing for solo piano, the piece wasn't that difficult to put together.

    The haunting, driving nature of the piece painted only one picture in my head: Rebecca's Enchantress ceremony. Wielding ancient draconian magic may seem desirable, but with it comes a crushing responsibility: keeping the peace between the human and dragon races, just as Rebecca's unbroken lineage has done countless times before her.

Listen here:
https://soundcloud.com/rldavennor/enchantress

Excerpt from *Bloodlust*, Chapter X. Enchantress

Sitora's wing shoved Rebecca face-first into the ocean before she had a chance to take a breath. The saltwater stung like poison, infiltrating her body where flesh had melted away. Rebecca spread her arms, the knowledge that she wasn't far from the surface keeping her from panicking. Water invaded her nostrils, flooding her open mouth as she kicked her legs, but she would not rise. A weight settled atop her, blocking her access to air. To life.

She gritted her teeth. Yet another sick, twisted test. Did they wish to see if she would fight? How long she could hold her breath? Perhaps some creature awaited her in the depths, drawn in by the scent of her blood mingling with the water. Rebecca no longer cared. She only wanted the nightmare to end.

There came a point where she could no longer ignore the tightness in her chest. She twisted, shoving against the force holding her down, but it did not budge. Did the dragons not realize she would drown? Rebecca flailed with all her strength as true terror set in. She screamed only to be met with more water filling her lungs.

Her mind grew hazy. She wanted air more than she'd ever wanted anything else. She choked on ocean water, sputtering as it stung her throat. After everything she'd endured, how could this be happening? Drowning was never how she imagined she would perish.

She surrendered when she could move no more. The darkness welcomed her with open arms, dissolving away her pain. Rebecca smiled. Soon she would be with Eleanor. She heard faint musical laughter beckoning her into the blackness, and the desire to go under soon overshadowed her desire for air.

Moments passed as Rebecca's body swayed with the tide. She hadn't emerged from the ocean, but neither had she gone beyond. Was this what death felt like? She no longer felt desperate for oxygen, but could not will herself to move.

Claws gripped her bare arms, ripping Rebecca from the waters. As fresh air struck her face, with it returned the painful reminder to breathe. Her chest heaved as the dragons roared, their cries stirring something deep within her soul.

She could not force her eyes open—not yet. Sitora cradled Rebecca in her wing as they made their way back to shore. Her brand stung, but not as much as before, and she realized the sea had already begun to heal the wound.

My child, you've done it. The first words Sitora had spoken since the ceremony began.

Now that she could breathe, Rebecca coughed the excess water from her lungs. *Haven't I died?*

You've done just the opposite. A true Enchantress of the ocean cannot drown.

It was pitch dark save for glowing draconian eyes. The crowd met them as their feet touched dry sand, surrounding Rebecca on all sides even as she leaned upon Sitora for support. They fell silent, parting to allow Eluth to approach. He regarded Rebecca through narrowed golden eyes before lowering his neck to the ground. One by one, the rest of the dragons followed suit.

"*The ocean has returned what we've given. As one Enchantress falls, another rises in her place.*"

Enchantress.

Rebecca shuddered, but not from the cold.

ENCHANTRESS

R. L. DAVENNOR

bring out melody - alternate whole notes for 8ths

The Execution

Scored for:

Pipe Organ   Snare Drum

Composed February 2020

I composed *The Execution* as I was working on a short story with the same title. I'd wanted to compose for solo pipe organ for as long as I'd been composing, and this piece could still work without the snare (which was really only added for effect). The music was crafted around the 16th note section played by the right hand starting in measure 24: a 'running' motif. The very beginning is meant to be reminiscent of a church hymn, which makes the ending that much more chilling, and the melody featured in the left hand is meant to embody desperation.

Laena is racing through the streets to stop an unjust execution. It is dusk, and many churches in her city are holding services at this hour. All she can hear is organ music as well as her own blood roaring in her ears as she prays to arrive in time to stop the proceedings. Included is an excerpt from earlier in the narrative, illustrating who Laena is and what she fights for.

Listen here:
https://soundcloud.com/rldavennor/the-execution

Excerpt from *Legends of Khovaa*, Chapter I. Laena

The warm, salty air sent a chill down Laena's spine. She checked her hood as she shuddered, making certain not a single wisp of hair showed beneath the dark, coarse fabric. Though she enjoyed her rare trips to the market, it had its drawbacks. It was a long way back to the Master's shop, and if her silver hair was spotted by the wrong person, quite a long way to flee.

As she weaved her way through the crowded and busy streets, wanting desperately to admire the colors and indulge in the local delicacies, she kept a careful and calculated distance. Laena was here for fresh air and to purchase supplies for Master, and she'd already done the latter. All that remained was to linger for the little free time she was afforded until she would be forced to return to her small and cramped room. She had even less than usual now that it had been announced an execution would take place later that evening; the merchants would be ordered to clear the square in just a few short hours.

A group of giggling children raced by, nearly causing her to drop the bundle Laena clutched to her chest. She shook her head in annoyance until she realized that one of the boys brazenly sported a head of ashen hair. He disappeared around a corner with his friends, but she didn't miss the hushed whispers lingering long after he passed.

Starchild. Those unfortunate enough to be born like her grew to adulthood just like anyone else, but earned their name because only a rare few survived their childhoods. There were many reasons for all the premature deaths, and as Laena followed the whispers, she discovered a stand that represented one of them.

The shopkeeper, who had been staring rather longingly at where the Starchild had disappeared, flashed her a toothy grin. "See anything ya like?"

"No, but I see plenty I *don't* like."

Laid before her in a grotesque display were human body parts. Most innocent were bundles of white hair and fragments of fingernails—most sinister was an array of decapitated fingers and toes. Several unseeing eyeballs stared back at her, packed in their own individual jars, and ready to be sold. Laena bit the inside of her lip as she took it all in. Beneath the folds of her cloak, her grip around her concealed dagger tightened.

"Genuine Starchildren parts, one hundred percent all-natural, and satisfaction guaranteed—"

"You need to leave. *Now.*"

Confusion crossed the shopkeeper's face before his lips curled into a chuckle. "Ah… You're a sympathizer. But I'm willing to bet you've never even given the parts a chance. Mine are the most potent you'll find in all of Marowe, never once have they failed a single one of my customers—"

Laena laid her parcel on the table and held up a hand to silence him, biting the inside of her lip to keep from snapping a venomous retort. *Never meddle in the affairs of humans.* She'd already put her one and only rule to the test by even approaching the man, and she had no indication of whether or not the parts were indeed as real as he said. Plenty of scheming merchants passed off counterfeits to turn a profit. Much as she loathed herself for asking, she forced the words through gritted teeth. "Prove it."

"I'd be delighted."

As she watched, the shopkeeper took a small handful of hair and sprinkled it rather dramatically into a shallow basin. He struck and lit a match, allowing Laena to see it burn the usual red and orange before dropping it straight into the container. A brilliant blue flame shot up, cool to the touch even while sparks danced over the hairs. Grinning wide, the shopkeeper waved his palm in and out of the fire, flexing his hand as a shudder passed through him.

"See? Genuine."

Something snapped within her. Laena trembled with rage, working hard to keep her voice even. "Where did you get these?"

"A good merchant never reveals his secrets."

"Are they from *children?*"

He smiled. "The parts are most potent when sourced from children."

"That's not a fucking answer," Laena snarled.

"That's a filthy word for such a pretty girl to know. Look, are ya interested in buying, or not?"

"I'll give you one more chance to get your ass *out* of here."

They eyed one another as, for the first time, the man's face fell. "Leave now, and miss the execution? I don't think so."

Laena was on him in an instant. Her free hand gripped the front of his tunic, yanking him over his disgusting wares while her blade dug into his throat, drawing a thin trail of blood. It took every ounce of restraint she possessed not to end his pathetic existence there and now.

"Perhaps you'd rather attend your own."

He struggled against her grip. "You don't know who you're dealing with—"

"No, *you* don't know who *you're* dealing with." Laena dug her blade in deeper, pressing down until the man sputtered and held his hands up in surrender.

"For Gods' sake, I yield!"

She shoved him back so hard he tumbled against the stack of crates behind him. The entire structure toppled, and he fell on his ass. Laena relished the sight of the wares being swallowed by the cloud of dust they'd kicked up. For good measure, she slung her arm across the counter, smashing open the jars and scattering the hair and fingernails.

Satisfied, she stepped back, wiping her bloodied dagger on her cloak before concealing it beneath the folds. Laena didn't realize her hood had fallen until a flash of silver caught her eye, nor did she hear the whispers until they surrounded her on all sides, inescapable and deafening.

"She's one of them."

Laena redrew her blade and whirled around, instinctively dipping into a feral crouch. A crowd of mostly men had her trapped—some merchants, some passersby, and even a few city guardsmen. She flicked her gaze between them, calculating her odds. With the lack of actual weapons, she *could* best them and make an escape, but not without revealing even more of her identity than she already had. Splintered wood and broken glass lay strewn at her feet, informing her she'd just broken her rule into a thousand visible pieces. Never meddle.

Shit.

THE EXECUTION

R. L. DAVENNOR

Fall of the Flowers

Scored for:

Low Whistle in D   *String Orchestra*
Koto

Composed February 2020

    Fall of the Flowers was more a challenge for myself than anything else. A friend approached me with a fun project: she aimed to write a short piece of writing based on nothing but an image, and my job became to write an equally short piece of music to embody her writing. I gave myself no longer than an hour, and aimed to keep the piece's performance time under a minute and thirty seconds.

    Her writing was dark, tragic, and with clear Asian influence, so I aimed to portray that through both the Koto and the melody in the whistle, with the added strings only for effect.

Listen here:
https://soundcloud.com/rldavennor/fall-of-the-flowers

Fall Of The Flowers

R. L. Davennor

Fallen Princess

Scored for:

Voice   *Lute*

Composed March 2020

I had no idea Alex could play an instrument, but she told me as I composed *Fallen Princess*. The music came before the scene, but once the music was done, I could picture what was happening in my head like a movie. It was incredibly tempting to have a more melodic instrument play the melody heard in the beginning, but I wanted as much solo lute as possible, as well as a 'song without words,' and I believe that I accomplished both.

The words sung by Rebecca at the end aren't the words Alex couldn't remember, but rather words Rebecca made up on the spot both to encourage and reassure her.

Listen here:

https://soundcloud.com/rldavennor/fallen-princess

Excerpt from *Bloodlust*, Chapter XVI. Pact

An hour later, she gritted her teeth as she plucked yet another wrong note on the lute. The dragons had gone off to hunt, so Alex sat away from Rebecca and Tristan, remaining close enough for her back to be warmed by the fire they'd built, but far enough away for the sounds of the forest to wrap her in their embrace. The tips of her fingers prickled uncomfortably, but she pressed on, determined to practice until she either bled or got it right—whichever came first.

"Remind me again why you brought a lute you can't even play?" Tristan glanced up from polishing his sword to shoot her a scowl. "The extra weight is slowing us down."

"I *can* play, it's just been a while." She nodded towards Tristan's sword. "And I promise you this 'extra weight' will come much more in handy than that ever could."

Tristan scoffed. "How? To make your enemies beg for you to stop?"

"*Tristan!*" Rebecca shot up, shaking her head and folding her arms.

"All I'm saying is that she'd be much better off crafting more arrows. Or sparring some more. *Something.* It's a romantic notion, but music isn't a weapon."

Alex stopped listening. Muscle memory kicked in, and she began to remember the tune she'd been searching for. Only after she'd plucked out most of the melody did she realize Rebecca had settled beside her, so close their arms brushed against one another.

"It's lovely," Rebecca said.

Alex was glad for the darkness concealing the heat that crept to her cheeks. "My father's favorite."

"You'll play it for him?"

"If he needs…persuading." Alex continued strumming, both exhilarated and terrified by Rebecca sitting so close. "The only problem is that I can't remember the words."

"Does it need them?"

Alex frowned. "It's how he's accustomed to hearing it."

"Try it without just to see how it sounds. Maybe he'll like it better."

Had anyone else made the suggestion, Alex would have told them you don't just go around changing the opinion of kings. But for Rebecca, Alex closed her eyes and allowed her fingers to do the rest. The strumming began clumsily and slow but soon picked up its pace. When it came time for the words she couldn't remember, Alex hummed instead, and for that brief span of time, it became just the two of them. Rebecca swayed back and forth to the rhythm of the song, her toes tapping the ground and her shoulder brushing against Alex's with every downbeat. When it came to its inevitable end, they were even closer than they were when they began.

Rebecca's voice rose from the silence, startling Alex as she sang to the previously wordless melody.

"Fallen princess, lead us, guide us,
as we face the throne
Fallen princess, dragons' Eldest
you are not alone."

Tears hovered at the corner of Alex's eyes. Rebecca's voice had rendered her both speechless and motionless.

"There. Words to your song."

The moment broken, Rebecca headed back towards Tristan and the fire, leaving Alex exactly how she'd promised not to.

Alone.

FALLEN PRINCESS

R. L. DAVENNOR

Far Across the Seas

Scored for:

2 Flutes	Tuba
2 Oboes	Cymbal
2 Clarinets in Bb	Voice
2 Bassoons	Celesta
4 Horns	String Orchestra
2 Trombones	

Composed September 2019

I began humming the melody to *Far Across the Seas* while at work one afternoon, and once I got home it became a race to write it down. This work grew into something much more cinematic than I intended, especially once the lyrics came into being, and I wanted to encapsulate Laena's emotions as she wrestles with the difficult decision of whether to leave her girls or stay to comfort them through their nightmares. Writing the inner orchestra parts was a challenge, but a welcome one, and I was still able to further develop the melody in the process.

Laena, a fugitive in hiding with several young girls in her care, must sneak out almost every night for reasons pertaining to the whole group's safety. It's beginning to wear on the youngest members, so to comfort them, Laena sings a lullaby she learned while growing up on the high seas.

Listen here:
https://soundcloud.com/rldavennor/far-across-the-seas

Excerpt from *Moontide*, Chapter I. Starchild

Y ou're leaving?"
Calliope stood in the open doorway watching Laena's every move.
"Child, you should be sleeping."
"I wanted to sleep with you."
Laena's heart shattered. She crossed the room barefoot, carrying her boots in her free hand. "You left Orela all alone—you know she has nightmares."
Calliope didn't protest when Laena lifted her into her arms. She yawned, wrapping her arms around Laena's neck and burying her face in her shoulder as they walked back down the hall. Laena almost considered staying—almost.
Calliope left the door to the children's room partially open, making a silent reentrance possible. Imani lay sprawled across her mattress with books spread all around her, one serving as her pillow as if she'd fallen asleep reading it. Orela remained in the exact same position Laena had left her, curled up and sucking on her knuckle.
When she went to pry Calliope's arms from her neck, the girl fussed. "Shh," Laena soothed. She propped Calliope up in her lap, rocking her gently. "Would you like me to sing for you?"
Calliope nodded. Laena cleared her throat before beginning, stealing a glance at the dark hallway. She didn't wish for anyone else to hear her voice.

"The tide is ever rising through the night
Silver waters bathed in restless light
Far across the seas
Together you and I will be
The storms will come and go, the rains will fall
Listen now and hear my silent call
Morning sings her song
And whispers 'my child, don't be long'.

Far across the seas
Together you and I will be."

Calliope drooped just enough that Laena was able to lay her down, covering her small frame with a thick blanket to keep away the chill. For good measure, she reached for the small wind-up music box she'd given the girls as a gift not long ago. As the high pitched chimes continued the song, Laena crept out the door, down the hall, and out of the house.

FAR ACROSS THE SEAS

R. L. DAVENNOR

Mor - ning sings her so - ng and whis-pers 'my child, don't be long'

Hyacinth

Scored for:

Voice   Harp
Oboe   Strings

Composed June 2019

Hyacinth is a rarity in that the music existed as a singular idea, and I actually struggled to find a theme I could put lyrics to (as I fully intended for this to be a vocal work). I turned to a topic that had always fascinated and never disappointed me when it came to inspiration—Greek mythology—and discovered the tale of Apollo and his lover, Hyacinthus.

Hyacinthus was a mortal man so handsome he attracted the attention of not only one, but two gods, and Zephyrus was jealous of the young man's relationship with Apollo. Zephyrus, the god of wind, made it so a discus thrown by Apollo struck Hyacinthus in the head, killing him instantly. Heartbroken, Apollo had a hyacinth bloom upon his young love's grave.

Lyrics:

A jealous breeze is blowing
as crimson stains the ground
Cold and still his lover lies
and in his tears, he drowns

A mortal's love is fleeting
and fate can't be undone
Flowers bloom upon his grave
in death, they will be one

'Alas!' he cries, pale blue eyes
A god can never die
He vows to remember always
the love that set his heart ablaze

Listen here:
https://soundcloud.com/rldavennor/hyacinth

Hyacinth

R. L. Davennor

Lyrics:

A jeal - ous breeze is blow - ing as crim - son stains the ground Cold and still his lo - ver lies and in his tears he drowns

pale blue eyes A god can ne – ver die He vows to re-mem – ber al – ways the love that set his heart a –

blaze

solo

mp

Kaos's Theme

Scored for:

2 Flutes	Timpani
2 Oboes	Vibraphone
2 Clarinets in Bb	Chimes
2 Bassoons	Snare Drum
4 Horns (2 offstage)	Bass Drum
2 Trumpets in Bb	Cymbal
2 Trombones	Harp
Tuba	String Orchestra

Composed April 2019

After the success to which I composed *Alexandria's Awakening*, I wanted to rise to the challenge of creating another fully orchestrated 'character theme.' Kaos's was much more of a struggle, but come it did, especially in the middle and ending sections. The offstage horns were such a specific image in my head, and if there are any of my pieces I'd love to be performed live one day, Kaos's Theme would be at the top of the list.

Kaos is a character in *Bloodlust*—an incredibly central one even though he doesn't appear until halfway through the novel—and his theme tells his backstory that's as tragic as the music. Born a mountain dragon with powerful wings and a love and adoration for the sky, all that was stripped from Kaos when he ended up a captive in King Richard's dungeons.

Listen here:
https://soundcloud.com/rldavennor/kaoss-theme

Excerpt from *Bloodlust*, Chapter XX. Unbroken

Both Rebecca and the mondrákon in front of her released a breath. A weight she'd never been aware she carried lifted from her shoulders when she met silver eyes so much brighter than his scales—black as the night sky devoid of stars—but at the slightest movement, they shimmered red. She was so mesmerized by his appearance that she hardly noticed his presence flooding her mind until it nearly overwhelmed her, but she was far from afraid. They continued to inhale and exhale as one, eyes matching the intensity of the other's glow. The final piece to arrive was his name.

Kaos.

Rebecca reached out, needing to touch him to be certain he was real. Horns sharp enough to slice through flesh and teeth longer than her arm reflected the flames dancing around them, but though Kaos's nostrils flared, his gaze never faltered.

She inched forward. At any moment, Kaos could run, or worse…rip her outstretched arm from her body. Rebecca's heart fluttered faster, but not from fear. He wouldn't hurt her. He *couldn't* hurt her. It didn't make sense and was far beyond explanation—he was a *mondrákon*.

But her soul knew she was staring at her other half.

The moment she made contact shocked them both. Kaos's scales were rough and jagged, but *warm*, and filled Rebecca with inexplicable comfort. She wanted so badly to let her touch linger, and may have considered it if not for the sudden darkness that washed over their conjoined minds.

Before she could recoil, he snapped.

It was a warning. Kaos staggered back, turning to reveal his right side, and Rebecca gasped. Hundreds of scars marred his body, more scales belonging to healed-over wounds than still-intact flesh. Around his neck, a ring had rubbed completely away—evidence of a collar. Though enormous by okedrákon standards, Kaos was small compared to the other mondrákons even with wings tucked against his sides. Flaps of loose skin battered by the breeze betrayed the final, gut-wrenching blow.

Kaos could not fly.

In the time she'd spent scrutinizing him, he'd been doing the same. The look in Kaos's eyes had changed, glassy orbs now somewhere far away as the darkness in Rebecca's mind refused to lift. She tried calling for him by repeating his name over and over in her thoughts, but a barrier had been erected…one she could not penetrate. The spines along his back bristled, his teeth bared, and talons raked the dirt in preparation for doing the same to her flesh.

Kaos charged directly at her throat.

Kaos's Theme

R. L. Davennor

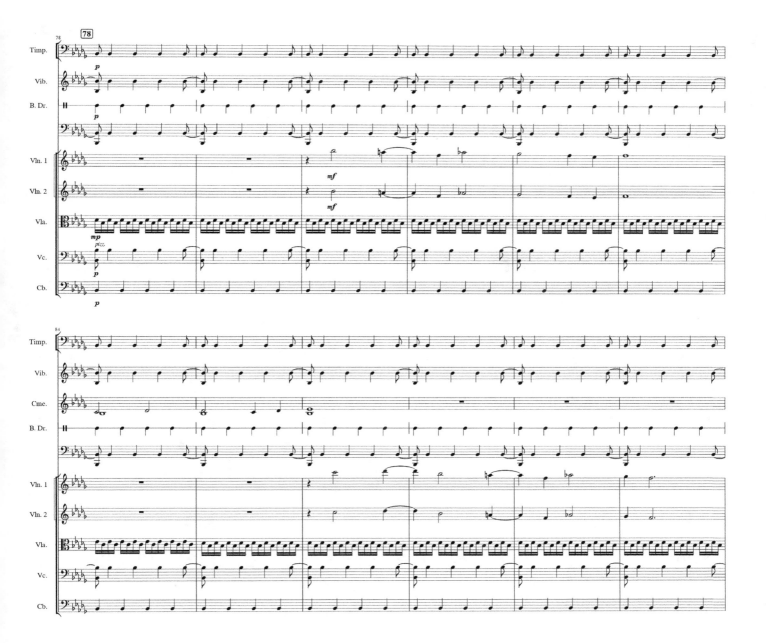

King's March

Scored for:

Piccolo	*Tuba*
Flute	*Timpani*
Oboe	*Snare Drum*
Clarinet in Bb	*Bass Drum*
Bassoon	*Harp*
4 Horns	*Bagpipes*
2 Trumpets	*String Orchestra*
2 Trombones	

Composed October 2019

I had a cinematic image in mind while composing *King's March*, rather than a specific moment or scene prepared with my writing. The music began with the ostinato line in the cellos, and I worked backward compared to how I usually operare, only composing the melody once I figured out the parts around it. Bagpipes were chosen to carry the tune not only for their volume, but for their regality; the oboe follows as an echo.

I envisioned the listener as a static entity, hearing the processions only once it appeared over the hill. The music would grow in volume as the parade drew closer, reaching its full height and depth in the middle where the orchestra plays the melody in tutti. As the parade departs, the instruments die away one by one, until all that's left are the cellos plucking their rhythmic ostinato much like the beat of a drum.

Listen here:
https://soundcloud.com/rldavennor/kings-march

King's March

R. L. Davennor

111

The Lover's Ballad

Scored for:

Voice	*Harp*
2 Piccolos	*String Orchestra*
Bass Flute	

Composed December 2018

This is a tune that also originated from my roleplaying days, though it wasn't ever paired with any scene I had actually written. Lovers and legends were fresh on my mind from having written endlessly about pirates for the past few months, so all I really aimed to do was compose a folk song that told both a story and a legend, which may or may not be true. The lyrics tell of a fated treasure hidden deep within a cave, as well as the tragedy that caused it to be hidden in the first place.

Lyrics:

Wandering the caverns old
Lovers both hands they hold
And in the night their secret told
Come morn, they grow cold

Turn back time and forget war
Forget the oath their fathers swore
These two souls who did adore
Whose hearts beat no more

Wandering the caverns old
Seek their graves and then behold
Brave the peril, it is foretold
Their hearts are made of gold

Listen here:
https://soundcloud.com/rldavennor/the-lovers-ballad

The Lover's Ballad

R. L. Davennor

told Their hearts are made of gold.

Ocean's Lullaby

Scored for:

Voice *String Orchestra*

Composed Summer 2018

Two versions of lyrics exist for this song, and that's because while it was originally composed for a role-play character as a lullaby his father used to sing to him, I entertained the possibility of the song appearing somewhere in my *Blood of the Covenant Trilogy*. Ultimately I decided against it, but the piece will always be special to me given its cinematic quality and the challenge that it was at the time to write the string parts.

Original Lyrics:

The winds the waves are howling
The sailors watch by night
Then come the morn they're drowning
As storm she takes her flight

The pirates spurned
The witches burned
The colors now they fly
All men must die
The crimson sky bleeds out
And moon soars high

The winds the waves are howling
The sailors watch by night
Then come the morn they're drowning
As storm she takes her flight

Modified Lyrics:

The winds the waves are howling
The men keep watch all night
Yet come the morn they're drowning
As dragons take their flight

The tides will rise
The children cry
The battle now is nigh
All life must die
The crimson sky bleeds out
And moon soars high

The winds the waves are howling
The men keep watch all night
Yet come the morn they're drowning
As dragons take their flight

Listen here:
https://soundcloud.com/rldavennor/oceans-lullaby

Ocean's Lullaby

R. L. Davennor

The winds the waves are howl - ing, the men keep watch all night Yet come the morn they're drown - ing as drag - ons take their flight. The tides will rise the child - ren cry the bat - tle now is nigh. All life must die the crim - son sky bleeds out and moon soars high. The

On Sacred Ground

Scored for:

Voice	*Bass Drum*
English Horn	*Cymbal*
Harp	*String Orchestra*

Composed July 2019

The main melody for this piece is, in part, a direct quote from the song *Misty Mountains* featured in the *Hobbit* movies. I created my own version of the tune, pairing with it a syllable pattern that happened to be a central phrase in *Bloodlust's* narrative: 'on sacred ground.' I treated the orchestration as a cinematic sequence in which the events of *Bloodlust's* prologue (by the same name) would play out during the instrumental sections, writing lyrics that were both tragic and poetic.

Just as the lyrics illustrate, the dragon Enchanters gather at the Gaea Tree for their monthly Translation, always held under a full moon, and always meant to be a truce. Vows are broken this fateful night, and many more than just the vow of peace.

Lyrics:
On sacred ground, they gather for the storm
To uphold vows that have been forsworn
Through wind and rain, the battle rages on
Until the dawn
Until the dawn

On sacred ground, her eyes betrayed us all
The blood will fall
The blood will fall

Listen here:
https://soundcloud.com/rldavennor/on-sacred-ground

Excerpt from *Bloodlust*, Prologue - On Sacred Ground

The clearing exploded into chaos.

Dragons turned on one another, human cries soon followed, and Elizabeth could barely catch her breath before Sidira slashed the poisoned knife across space she had occupied only moments ago. There was no time to make sure Alex heeded her warning. Elizabeth's form rippled back into view a little at a time—no use wasting precious energy when her enemy couldn't see—but it made no difference. Sidira fought just as well, if not better, than a sighted warrior, nostrils flaring and ears on high alert to guide her through smell and sound. Just as she'd been trained. She dodged the few strikes Elizabeth aimed at her, and it wasn't long before Sidira was on the offensive, blade weaving through the air with alarming speed.

A little help over here! It took immense concentration for Elizabeth to call for Sitora. Her dragon was close, but occupied with her own fight—Luke's dragon, Lykaer, had turned on her. Elizabeth gasped as she felt a sharp pain in her shoulder, indicating that Lykaer landed a nasty bite.

She was on her own.

Sidira took full advantage of Elizabeth's hesitation, grazing the knife across her upper elbow. The poison took immediate effect and her skin seared as if it were on fire, burning even in the cool night air. Elizabeth gritted her teeth and withdrew the limb back to her body, mind racing as she searched for a way out. She could shift into a fox, but she would not abandon Sitora.

"Surely it would be easier to kill me as a dragon—or have you allowed your emotions to hold you captive?" Elizabeth hissed in draconian, backing herself against a tree and hoping Sidira would take the bait.

Sidira snarled and plunged her blade into the tree trunk, the noise sounding more beast than human. Turning her unseeing face in Elizabeth's direction, she yanked and twisted, working to free the blade now stripped of most of its poison. "Don't you *dare* defile our tongue with your traitorous lips. I understand yours perfectly."

Elizabeth stilled as Sidira's words took root in her mind. A dragon in human skin speaking the human tongue—surely this had to be a first. "You've been busy all these years. Was this really the best plan you could devise? Attacking on sacred ground, on the night of a truce?"

Sidira laughed—another noise which shot a chill up Elizabeth's spine—as she freed her weapon from the tree. "I'm blind and yet have no trouble seeing through your lies. Look around—you weren't the only one to smuggle in a weapon."

Elizabeth turned her head just enough to hear the clashing of metal on metal. Kia and Luke were a whirlwind of silver and black—how in spirits' sake had they managed to conceal *swords?* Alex nor her dragon were anywhere to be found, which appeared to be the only shred of hope. The three remaining dragons writhed and thrashed in a chaotic cloud of teeth and claws, blood already staining the Gaea Tree's roots as it gathered in a single river of crimson. The battle cast eerie shadows over the clearing as the blazing fire burned stronger than ever.

"You're not here for me. You preyed on our distrust for one another." Elizabeth's knees grew weak as madness unfolded before her eyes.

"Let's not get ahead of ourselves," Sidira spat. "I *am* here for you."

ON SACRED GROUND

R. L. DAVENNOR

Rebecca's Theme

Scored for:

2 Flutes	*Glockenspiel*
2 Oboes	*Chimes*
2 Clarinets in Bb	*Congas*
2 Bassoons	*Bass Drum*
4 Horns	*Tambourine*
2 Trombones	*Harp*
Tuba	*String Orchestra*
Timpani	

Composed January 2019

Rebecca's Theme was originally composed as part of a larger orchestral work, but I liked this section so much I scored it to stand alone. Many elements of the music remind me of her: the dancelike rhythm of the 9/8 time signature, the melodic ostinato introduced in the harp, and the depth and darkness provided once the lower voices enter. I include oboe into so many of my pieces for the simple fact that I am an oboist, but for Rebecca, the singing, haunting quality of the oboe matches and represents her perfectly.

Rebecca is the protagonist both of *Bloodlust* and of the *Blood of the Covenant Trilogy*. She is headstrong, independent, stubborn, and abrasive when she has to be—qualities off-putting to many—but beneath all that, loyal, gentle, and loves with the ferocity of a dragon.

Listen here:
https://soundcloud.com/rldavennor/rebeccas-theme

Excerpt from *Bloodlust*, Chapter I. Consequences

It wasn't long before the trees parted to reveal the modest dwelling that made her heart swell every time she looked at it. Sporting misshapen stones, a low thatched roof, and wattle poking out from cracks that weren't quite sealed, it would make anyone accustomed to the comforts of the city turn up their nose in disgust. But to Rebecca, it symbolized Tristan's independence, and their friendship.

More than that now, she supposed. Words they whispered between kisses didn't erase what they'd done in the night. She approached the door and swallowed, fingers clenching around the still-warm body of the rabbit. With one final glance at the forest, she pushed the door open with her shoulder, smiling as she held up her prize.

She was greeted with an eerie silence.

The house consisted of a single room. Coals smoldered in the fireplace, and a candle had been lit next to the bed. The sheets lay disheveled, with still-wet clothes tossed in haphazard heaps on the floor. Rebecca's eyes flickered to where Tristan kept his cloak and boots. Gone, along with his sword. Irrefutable evidence he didn't plan to return for some time.

With chattering teeth, Rebecca slammed the door and laid the rabbit across the empty space on the table. It took her a moment to notice the yellowed parchment sticking out from beneath its tail. She squinted to make out Tristan's gibberish, hands shaking with something else entirely by the time she finished the simple sentence.

If you change your mind, you know where to find me.
-T

It was all she could do not to hurl the message into the fire. The very notion of *changing her mind* implied choice, something that had been denied to Rebecca—*and* Tristan—from the moment they were born. What imbecile with a *choice* would choose to live here, in the middle of nowhere and far away from the protection of the city? Such was their punishment for existing, and the punishment they were still paying for their ancestors' involvement with dragons. *Dragon-touched.* Spat like a dirty word and whispered under the breath of anyone who caught a glimpse of the glowing eyes that were the only evidence of the dragonsblood flowing through their veins, she'd heard it all her life. Full-blooded humans had the luxury of changing their minds and the freedom to make their own choices.

Rebecca could only hope the orders she was given to follow were kind.

Rebecca's Theme

R. L. Davennor

RUNNING

Scored for Solo Piano

Composed Summer 2013

Running is a piece I composed before I knew I was a composer. I set out to create a love theme for a roleplay I was participating in, and over and over the C-Db motif repeated in my head. I tinkered endlessly with the left hand and spent hours at the piano, using my own limited ability at the time to craft something pleasing to my ear rather than notating anything by hand. This piece didn't exist in a written form until I notated it for this collection, working off a recording of myself at the piano back in the same year it was composed.

The title *Running* comes from the cat and mouse back-and-forth the characters in question kept playing, running away from their feelings rather than embracing them head on. However, eventually, they ran to one another, finding comfort in their deepest hour of need.

Listen here:
https://soundcloud.com/rldavennor/running

Running

R. L. Davennor

Sidira's Theme

Scored for:

Oboe	*Zither*
English Horn	*Field Drum*
Harp	*Bass Drum*

String Orchestra Composed January 2020

Sidira is one of the most tragic characters I've ever written, and though she's not driven by forces of good, she's a victim of circumstance more than anything else. In many ways, she is the foil of Rebecca as well as a main antagonistic force, but in many other ways, they are the same. It's how I knew that when composing *Sidira's Theme*, the musical reflection had to personify this relationship as well as the two opposing forces within Sidira herself.

First, the key center: *Sidira's Theme* is in C# minor, only a half step up from *Rebecca's Theme* that exists in C minor. Both utilize solo oboe to state the melody. Both are written in triple meter, but *Sidira's Theme* has a twist: to musically illustrate the opposing forces within her, hemiola can be heard throughout the piece. A duple meter first begins in the cello and continues until it's heard in nearly every other instrument as well, but the zither persists with triple meter. The final tragedy of the piece occurs at the very end when the English Horn takes up the melody, and she and the oboe sing in a final lament to the end.

Listen here:
https://soundcloud.com/rldavennor/sidiras-theme

Excerpt from *Bloodlust*, Chapter VI. Nightmares

Sidira growled. With a final caress, she tore herself from Kaos and reluctantly turned her attention to Luke. He'd been shot twice by that scheming wench Alex—once in his back, a clean shot straight through—and once in his front. The shaft of the embedded arrow had been broken to ease Luke's movements, but the tip remained buried in his flesh. Sidira hadn't missed the way he'd been favoring his left side even in their long flight, and when he removed his shirt, the stench of infection flooded her nostrils. When Luke finished she extended her hands for him to take them in his own, guiding them to where the arrow tip rested.

"You're a fool—you *had* to know that already festered."

Behind them, Lykaer released a snarl that reverberated along the cavern walls. She continued speaking in the mondrákon tongue until Luke cut her off with a snappy retort.

"It's not wise to silence your dragon," Sidira warned as she reached for the knife, and sure enough, Lykaer was not finished, and even Kaos joined in the fray. Raised draconian voices soon filled the entirety of the hollow space. The mondrákon language was a harsh, peckish one, and Sidira hated the way it felt against her ears. She shook her head, but they continued their banter right up until she pressed the blade against Luke's bare chest.

"I don't recall saying I was ready," he hissed in the common tongue.

"I don't recall asking."

Luke tried to lower Sidira's hands, but she held firm. "Perhaps I should get a healer to look at this."

"No," Sidira snarled. "I mean... *Yes*, you need a healer, but you had every opportunity to do so. You could have ventured into Ide and sought one out—"

"And leave you alone? Not a chance."

Sidira's grip on the knife tightened. "I am *not* helpless."

Luke sighed. "You're not. But neither of us knew what would happen once *she* was dead."

She felt a stabbing pain in her gut. They managed to go nearly a day without mentioning Elizabeth, and the agony was still far too fresh. Bold, brazen even, for Luke to mention her while Sidira held a knife to his chest.

Gutting him would be far too easy.

"For spirit's sake, just *do* it already."

Fueled by her rage, Sidira did.

Luke gasped as she drove the blade forward. His flesh parted as easily as ocean waves and Sidira was guided only by what she could feel. She needed first to enlarge the wound before she could pry the arrow from its pocket of infection and fluid, without cutting herself in the process. Leaning in, she ignored Luke's grunts of discomfort as she fought to get a better grip on the broken shaft.

"Let...l-let me—"

"The last time I *let* you do anything, you stole my kill," Sidira growled. Blood coated her free hand as she twirled her thumb over the wound she'd made, fingers slipping in the slick conditions. Not large enough yet. "Rag."

Luke obeyed with quivering hands—perhaps she should have ordered him to lie down. The cloth soaked up enough for her to continue, and she propped it beneath the knife still holding back a flap of skin. She furrowed her brow, knowing he would have a gaping wound that would need stitching closed.

"You... y-you're the one who lied to me."

Sidira's grip faltered as she attempted to twist the shaft. She snapped her head up, forcing Luke to gaze into hollow sockets pointedly lacking her prosthetic eyes. "I'm sorry—would you rather I have told you the woman you loved never existed?"

His voice was hoarse. "She existed, just not—"

"Nora. Wasn't. Real. You slept with Elizabeth, and that sure as fuck wasn't love. That was treachery."

"I-If I had known—*AH!*"

Sidira plunged her thumb into Luke's chest. Sickening squelching and popping noises became all she could hear as she fished around, setting her jaw when she felt the jagged edges of the stone. Hooking her thumb around the tip of the arrow, she pulled, allowing the knife to clatter to the ground so her free hand could tug on the shaft. Several swift yanks were all it took. Luke swore and Lykaer screeched as Sidira kept hold of her prize, tracing her hands over the expert craftsmanship when the arrow finally came loose. She heard Luke stagger back, breathing shallow and fingers scraping against stone. In her chest, pain coursed through her veins with each beat of her own heart, spreading like venom.

It wasn't nearly enough to feel remorse at his suffering.

Sidira's whisper echoed along the chamber. "If you had known, you'd have killed her years ago."

"You were protecting her… even after everything she's done?"

"I was protecting *my* chance at freedom. You stole that from me."

Luke sighed, hesitating before he spoke. "Sidira… I cannot steal what you never had."

Sidira's Theme

R. L. Davennor

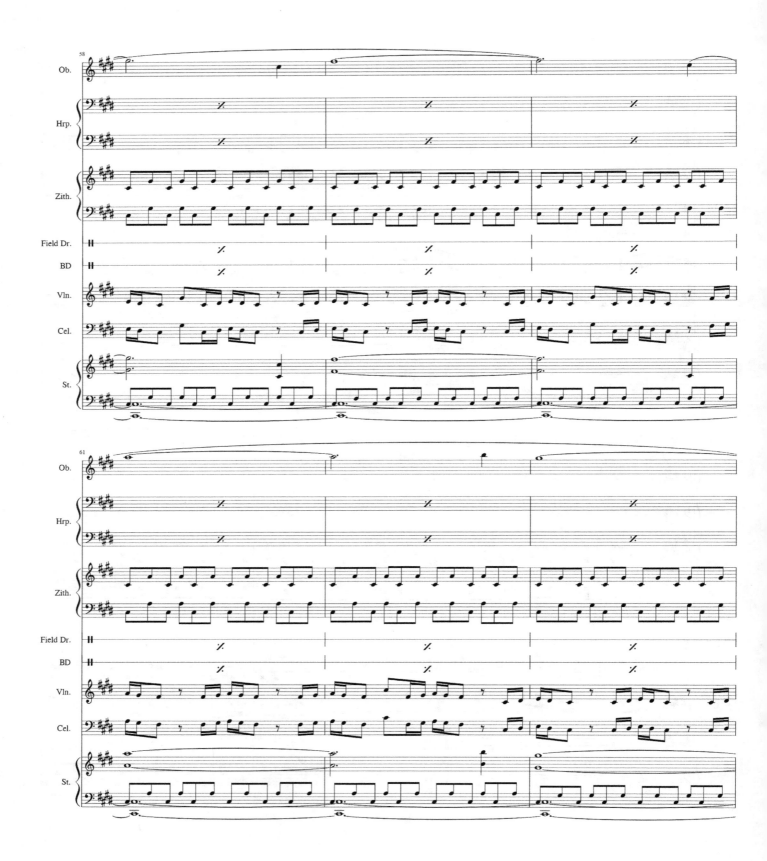

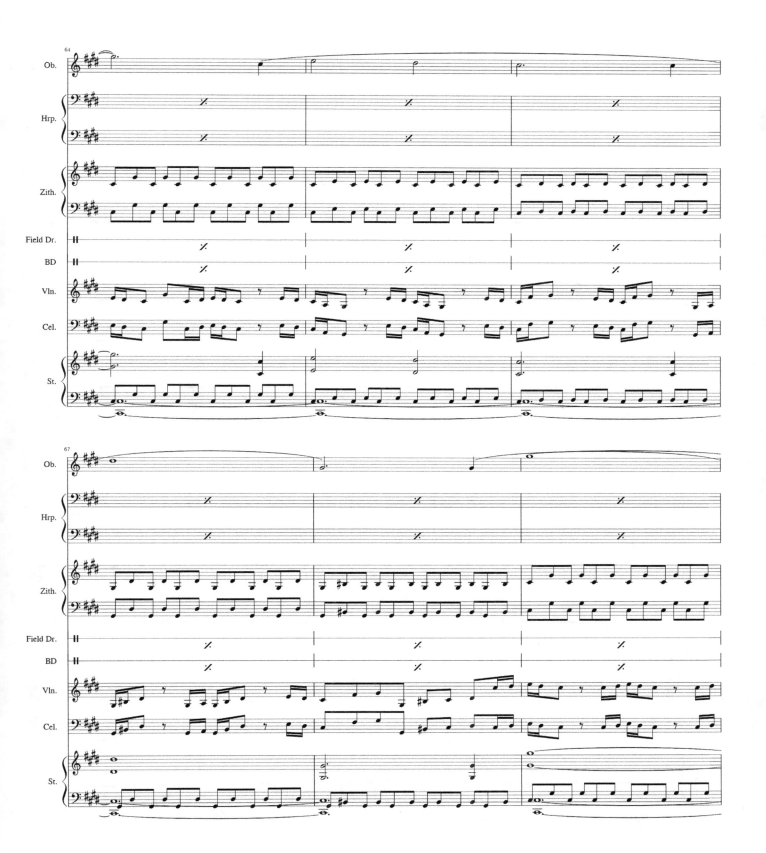

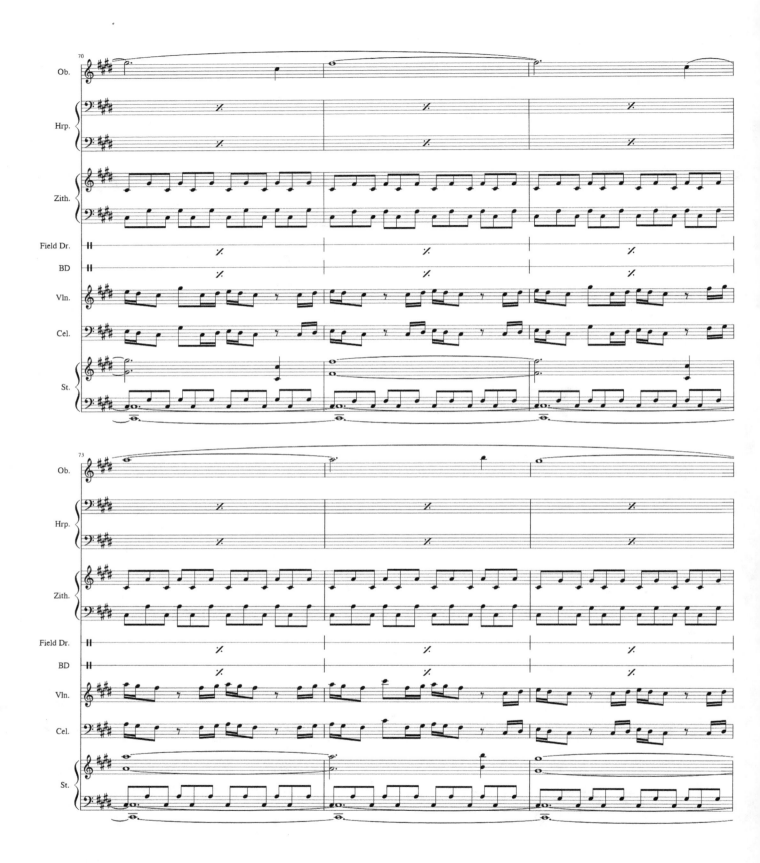

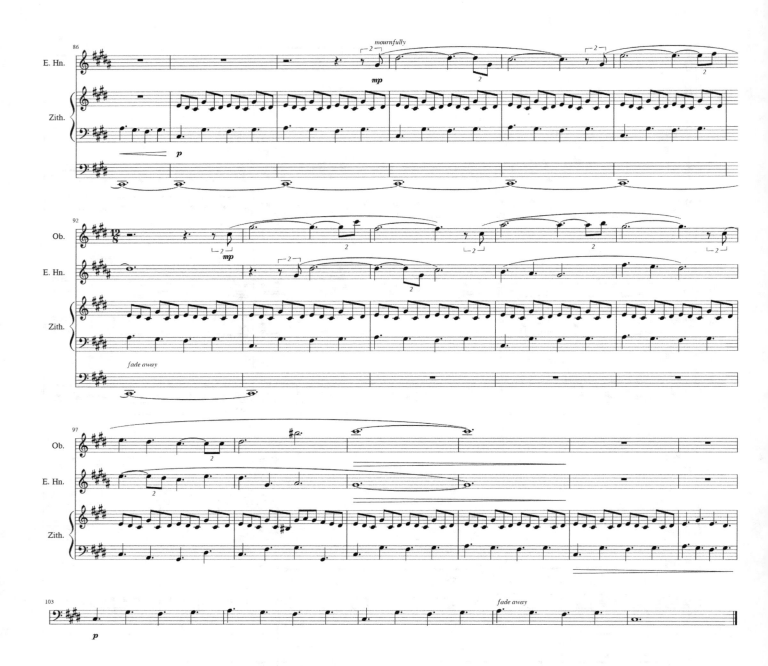

Soren's Song

Scored for:

Voice   String Orchestra
Harp

Composed May 2019

Soon after I really got comfortable with songwriting, *Soren's Song* came into being, and it remains one of my favorites in both lyrics and tune. Musically, it utilizes my favorite key center (Bb minor) and gorgeous, intentional simplicity. There is a specific scene and character (hence the title) I had in mind while composing this, but due to certain things not being published at the time I'm writing this, I'm electing to keep just who Soren is a secret for right now.

The lyrics themselves serve as both prophecy and vows, the latter of which are spoken when a new Enchanter makes a blood pact with the Gaea Tree. The section beginning 'dragonsblood born anew' is a prediction which comes to pass in *Bloodbound*, the sequel to *Bloodlust*.

Lyrics:
Born of ash, cloaked in fire,
broken free of man's desire
branded flesh by searing claw
Straight into the gaping maw

Bones will snap, wills can bend
Storms will pass and journey's end
Ebb and flow, give and take
The strongest heart will never break

Dragonsblood born anew
A shroud of green and cloak of blue
Shadowed wings rise and fall
Stolen child, free us all.

Listen here:
https://soundcloud.com/rldavennor/sorens-song

Excerpt from *Bloodlust*, Chapter XVI. Pact

Still your breathing. Calm your mind. However it is you summon your power, do it now."

And then she waited.

Seven years of honing her abilities meant that Alex could call forth her healing without a second thought, but these two had been allotted barely three weeks. It was unfair of her to force Rebecca into shifting earlier, but she'd been curious at how advanced her magic was, especially considering her impressive mastery of language. The sildrákon tongue had given Alex far more trouble than her magic, but for Rebecca, it seemed to be the opposite.

Tristan didn't take long to call forth his magic and doubled over once he was done, but not so much that Alex couldn't see the sweat forming on his brow. "How long must I hold it?" he forced through gritted teeth.

Rebecca was having no such luck. She held out her hands, clenching and unclenching her fists as if she hoped to snatch power from thin air, but there was nothing. No shimmering of her form, and none of the sensation Alex was accustomed to feeling around Elizabeth when she shifted.

Alex offered a warning. "Rebecca, the Tree will not accept you without an offering—"

"I'm fucking trying," Rebecca growled. She opened her eyes, pointedly lacking a glow, and groaned. Her disappointment shot a chill down Alex's spine.

She shouldn't interfere—it was against the rites. If Rebecca was meant to fail, there was absolutely nothing she could do to prevent it, and ultimately, the Tree's decision was one that could not be swayed.

But watching Rebecca struggle was intolerable.

Alex reached into the circle to grip Rebecca's shoulder, offering the same squeeze she'd given her wrist, and the effect on both was immediate. The Tree's power surged through Alex's blood, setting it aflame while Rebecca threw her head back and gasped, no doubt feeling the same thing. She didn't begin to shift but radiated a different type of energy the moment her green eyes began to glow enough for the ritual to continue.

"Blood…*now!*"

Alex didn't dare break her hold on Rebecca as she reached for her dagger, tossing it into the space between Rebecca and Tristan. He snatched it first, positioning the blade against his palm and slicing without hesitation. While his hand dripped with crimson, he placed it flat against the Tree's bark, shuddering as he too felt its power.

Once Rebecca followed suit, Alex pulled the words of the pact from where they'd settled deep within her soul, instructing the new Enchanters to repeat after her.

> "Born of ash, cloaked in fire,
> Broken free of man's desire
> Branded flesh by searing claw
> Straight into the gaping maw.
>
> Bones will snap, wills can bend
> Storms will pass and journeys end
> Ebb and flow, give and take
> The strongest heart will never break."

Palms pressed against the tree, Rebecca and Tristan spoke the solemn vow. Around them, the forest stilled, and even the dragons settled down to wait until it was done. While they waited for the Tree's verdict, Alex sank to her knees without releasing Rebecca.

She couldn't.

SOREN'S SONG

R. L. DAVENNOR

born a-new a shroud of green and cloak of blue Sha - dowed wings rise and fall

Sto - len child free us all

STARLIGHT

Scored for:

Piano	*Timpani*
2 Flutes	*Bass Drum*
Oboe	*Cymbal*
Bassoon	*Harp*
Tuba	*String Orchestra*

Composed May 2019

Another of my earliest 'serious' compositions, *Starlight* remains a favorite. I drew heavy inspiration from Hans Zimmer and the *Interstellar* soundtrack as I began crafting the piano and harp parts together, utilizing the same rhythmic ostinatos and melodic drones heard in the most well-known tracks from the movie.

Unlike many of my other compositions of the time, I didn't have any scene or character in mind from my writing: just the image of a clear night sky. The interweaving of the two different melodies originally introduced by the oboe was completely unintentional, but worked brilliantly and helped drive the music to its triumphant, yet tragic climax.

Listen here:
https://soundcloud.com/rldavennor/starlight

Starlight

R. L. Davennor

Stone Maiden

Scored for:

Voice   *12 String Guitar*
Oboe   *String Orchestra*

Composed June 2019

    Stone Maiden was never intended to be a song nor a vocal piece. The introduction was written long before the rest of the work as a standalone I wasn't sure how to incorporate into a more complete piece, and I envisioned it belonging to something entirely instrumental. However, once the guitar part and vocal melody was written, I found that the oboe melody of the introduction worked as a way to hold everything together.

    The lyrics tell the story behind a statue of a maiden erected in the Royal Gardens. Alexandria has always found herself fascinated by the legend behind it, and sings the folk tune to her companions one night around a fire.

Lyrics:
On the water clear as glass
dances light of the moon
His love lies still and pale
taken from him too soon

His tears have all run dry
The birds have fallen silent in the sky
He won't leave her alone
he stays until she is stone.

On the water clear as glass
dances light of the moon

Listen here:
https://soundcloud.com/rldavennor/stone-maiden

STONE MAIDEN

R. L. DAVENNOR

On the wa - ter clear as glass   dan-ces light   of   the   moon

fade away

Storm Dance

Scored for:

Whistle in D	*Guitar*
Fiddle	*2 Bodhrans*
Hurdy Gurdy	*Hand Clap*

Composed April 2020

I was playing around with a guitar melody the night this was composed, and hadn't set out to write a dance. However, as soon as I added a rhythmic fiddle ostinato, the piece took off from there. Taking advantage of traditional Celtic and folk instruments, I did my best to keep the tune lively, catchy, and spirited.

I began to imagine a stormy night aboard the *Rogue*, Laena Myatt's flagship. She and her girls are huddled below deck, sharing stories and attempting to calm the children, but it doesn't work. Laena reaches for her fiddle, establishes a rhythm, and it's not long before the other musicians aboard the ship join her. Soon they're all laughing and dancing, but as the song draws to a close, the storm remains, the music only having served as a temporary distraction.

Listen here:

https://soundcloud.com/rldavennor/storm-dance

STORM DANCE

R. L. DAVENNOR

175

A Study in Anger

Scored for Solo Piano

Composed May 2020

I wish I could say I had nobler intentions when I composed this piece, but the truth is this: I was angry, and needed an outlet. Solo piano was an interesting choice, especially for me and my background, but for some reason it fit. The repetitive motif is meant to represent my nagging thoughts and their insistence throughout, while the singular notes struck in the left hand give a feeling of ambiguity. The piece follows a circular pattern, beginning and ending calmly while swelling and reaching climax in the middle.

I selected the title both as a nod to the emotions I felt while composing it, but also as a nod to the etudes many musicians are taught as a child.

Listen here:
https://soundcloud.com/rldavennor/a-study-in-anger

A Study in Anger

R. L. Davennor

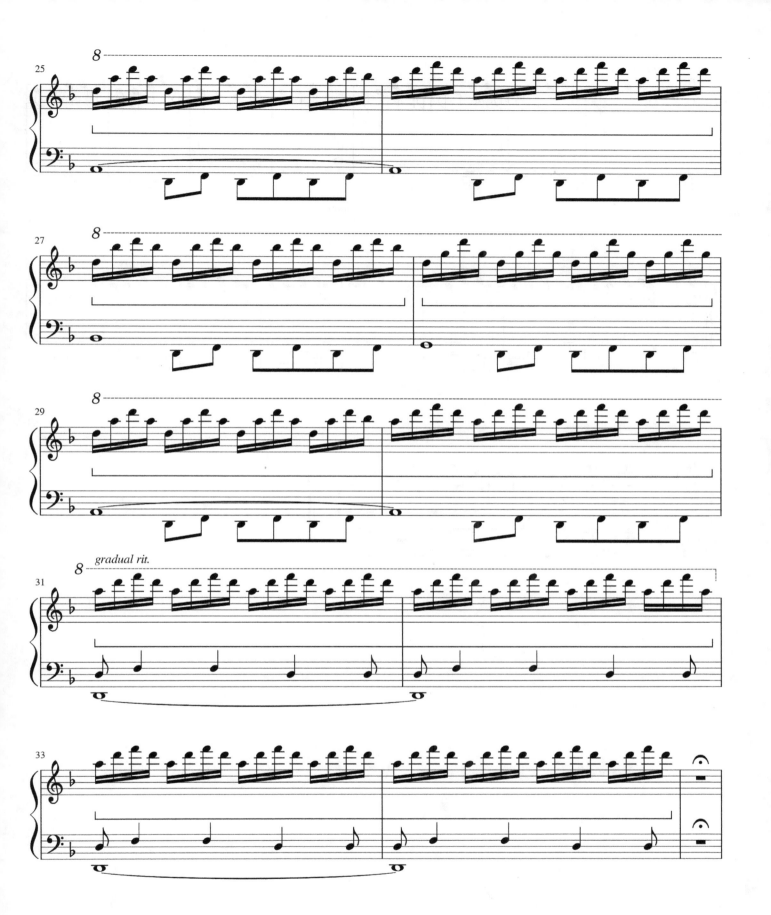

179

To the Castle

Scored for:

Oboe	*Congas*
English Horn	*Bass Drum*
Guitar	*Cymbal*
Harp	

Low Strings Composed July 2019

To the Castle is a piece where everything just fell into place. At the point it was composed, I hadn't written much for guitar, and that's where I started playing around with a simple melody. Add drums and the quarter note ostinato, and a cinematic 'traveling' piece was born. The mood perfectly encapsulated Rebecca's emotions as she is on the way to the castle for her marriage to William Shiel, the son of her village lord. In addition to the dark, broody theme in the oboe and guitar, I also include a more playful theme in the English Horn, which both complements the existing material and subverts expectations for the instrument; usually heard singing lament-like melodies, and hardly ever showing the lighter side of itself.

Listen here:
https://soundcloud.com/rldavennor/to-the-castle

Excerpt from *Bloodlust*, Chapter I. Consequences

Eleanor had fallen asleep a mile back, and so had Rebecca's arm. The guard had never taken his eyes from either of them. Once she'd grown bored of imagining all the different ways she could pry her knife beneath his armor, Rebecca considered asking him if he'd like a demonstration of her shifting prowess. She'd never manifested a shred of such magic, but he didn't need to know that.

Her draconian gift was more like a curse. Rebecca managed to keep her visions at bay thus far but left to the mercy of her own thoughts, she didn't know how much longer she'd be able to hold out. They were the reason she'd never once had a peaceful night's rest, though her waking hours offered no protection. It would be one thing if she could feign sleep once a vision took hold, but the unlucky few who had witnessed her spells assured her they were terrifying. Her eyes rolled back in her head, she whispered in chant, her body crumpled, and she was a captive until the vision passed.

The pulsing in her head grew stronger with each passing moment. Rebecca clenched her fists as sweat gathered at her brow, fighting an internal battle more difficult than any spar she'd ever had with Tristan.

The guard didn't take long to notice. "My lady, you don't look well."

"Stop the carriage." Rebecca peeled herself from Eleanor, lying her across their seat and praying she wouldn't wake. Even though Rebecca could hardly see through the black spots dancing across her field of vision, she stood.

"Sit down—"

"STOP!" Rebecca screamed as she fumbled with the latch, relief flooding through her as the door swung open. With the carriage still in motion, she leaped to freedom, knees buckling to absorb the impact.

She heard voices shouting her name, but her mind already straddled two worlds. Flames drifted into the night sky while swords clashed and the overwhelming scent of blood consumed her psyche.

I am here for you.

The voice was unlike any other she'd ever heard. Rebecca's mind worked to sear it into her memory while arms shook her body like a ragdoll, causing the vision to grip her even tighter. Draconian screeches deafened her ears to all other noise, and her chest heaved as she fought to draw breath. She tasted blood on her tongue, and whether it belonged to her or the corpses strewn across her vision, she couldn't be sure.

A blinding pain on her cheek snapped Rebecca to the present. She blinked in the afternoon sunlight, coming to the realization that she'd been slapped across the face.

"What are you doing?!"

Eleanor's cry had Rebecca fully conscious in an instant. The carriage guard gripped her cousin's arms even as Eleanor screamed and thrashed.

Rage boiled beneath Rebecca's skin as she made a move to stand. "Don't fucking touch her—"

A second strike sent her right back to the ground. Rebecca's teeth clicked together, clipping the inside of her cheek in the process. Head spinning and palms trembling, it was some time before she could see straight, let alone pull herself upright. Blood trailed from her lip while the dress that cost so much now sported muddy stains.

The man who had struck her spat on the ground in front of her. "We don't take orders from women."

Rebecca shot him a murderous glare, fully aware of the knife hidden in her boot. If Eleanor hadn't been present, she wouldn't have hesitated to use it. "William will punish you for this."

"A copper says he'll thank me. Unless you'd like to be sporting a black eye for your wedding, I suggest getting back in the carriage."

Rebecca didn't move.

"All right then—*she* gets a black eye. Makes no difference to me."

She shot forward before the guard finished speaking. Once back inside the carriage, a sobbing Eleanor was deposited into Rebecca's lap, and the door slammed and bolted in both of their faces. As they started forward, the throbbing pain in Rebecca's skull was nothing compared to the tightness gripping her chest. This was exactly why William had insisted Eleanor tag along. No longer could Rebecca set a toe out of line.

Not while there was a chance Eleanor might pay the price.

To The Castle

R.L. Davennor

The Wailing Caverns

Scored for:

Soprano
Mezzo-soprano
Alto
Soprano Ocarina

Lute
Guitar
String Orchestra

Composed February 2020

This tune was born solely because I had recently taken up the ocarina and wanted to use it. I adored the piercing sound of the soprano version in particular, and couldn't stop envisioning how it might sound echoing in a mysterious cavern prone to flooding. The lyrics tell the unfortunate and tragic tale of three young maidens who drowned here at high tide. Legends whisper you can still hear their wailing, and this is what the ocarina is meant to imitate. The spirits remain hungry for revenge and lure men to their graves at any given opportunity.

I am hopeful that I will be able to include this work somewhere in the *Godsworn* trilogy once it's published.

Lyrics:
Down by where the waters flow
Three young maidens fled
Following the river that
now runs red.

And they cried oh, oh, oh
Oh, oh oh.
Dresses torn and feet all bare
They all held their breath
High tide came, and with the night
So did death

And they cried oh, oh, oh
Oh, oh oh.
Spirits wander aimlessly
on the hunt for blood
Men are lured into their graves
when they flood

And they cried oh, oh, oh
Oh, oh oh.

Listen here:
https://soundcloud.com/rldavennor/the-wailing-caverns

The Wailing Caverns

R. L. Davennor

Spi - rits wan - der aim - less - ly on the hunt for blood Men are lured in -

A Warrior's Heart

Scored for:

Voice   *High Strings*
Lute

Composed September 2019

I wanted more practice composing for lute and in turn gave myself a challenge: to compose a tune that told a complete story with its lyrics. I used the fantasy genre itself as inspiration rather than a specific scene from my own stories, so here is my take on the 'woman waiting for her knight to save her.' True to my nature as a storyteller, and unfortunately for our maiden, she's in for a tragedy.

Lyrics:
Maiden fair in silken dress
longing for her love's caress
even though they're worlds apart
she will keep her warrior's heart

Seasons change, the leaves turn red
word comes that the war has spread
bitter winds blow, the birds depart
she waits for her warrior's heart

Oooo…

Fallen snow, a soldier lost
buried in the deepest frost
never will he make it home
his lone soul forever roams

Oooo…

Maiden pale in tattered dress
all she feels is emptiness
left alone, she fell apart
waiting for her warrior's heart

Listen here:
https://soundcloud.com/rldavennor/a-warriors-heart

A Warrior's Heart

R. L. Davennor

A Wayward Storm

Scored for:

2 Voices	*Bass Drum*
Men	*Cymbal*
Timpani	*Low Strings*

Composed October 2019

As much as I wanted to compose a deep and dark sea shanty that a crew of men could bellow, it's difficult for me to imagine as well as demonstrate for myself. Regardless, I took on such a challenge with *A Wayward Storm*, another phrase I fell in love with after writing a chapter with the same name.

Laena, a pirate captaining a highly inexperienced crew, jumps overboard during a storm to save a man she's fallen in love with—Zareen. They manage to wash ashore on a small island, and after patching up each other's wounds, they make love. While waiting for rescue, Zareen asks Laena to sing, and having been raised on a ship herself, this is the tune she chooses.

Listen here:
https://soundcloud.com/rldavennor/a-wayward-storm

Excerpt from *Riptide:* Sequel to *Moontide*

They reached their destination and settled in the sand just out of reach of the tide. Laena hugged her knees and stared at the foamy waves, unwilling to scan the horizon to see if she could make out any sign of imminent rescue. She'd never admit it out loud, but she wasn't ready to leave.

"Any ideas to pass the time?" Zareen's voice broke her self-imposed trance.

"Mine was to sit here in silence, but I forgot that's impossible for you."

"I just need...a distraction."

Laena glanced over and softened when she saw Zareen's fingers tugging on his sleeve. "Unfortunately for both of us, *that* type of distraction is off the table—"

"I wasn't talking about that." He continued his fidgeting. "I was wondering...if you might sing for me?"

Caught off guard, Laena frowned. "I don't sing."

"Yes you do. I've heard you putting the girls to bed."

Unable to think of a way out, Laena scowled. "Fine—but I pick the song."

Zareen nodded.

"You won't like it."

"Somehow I doubt that."

Laena expelled all the air from her lungs before taking a deeper breath. She'd only sung when certain she was alone or when her audience was drifting off to sleep, unless part of a larger group where individual voices were impossible to make out. Shanties, especially the old ones, were her favorite, and sadly lacking aboard the *Rogue* with her girls not having been raised on the high seas. Laena cleared her throat before beginning. At first, her voice was soft as though she were singing a lullaby to lull Calliope to sleep, but as she reached the chorus, she bellowed as if an entire crew backed her.

"A wayward storm upon the sea
Star-filled skies are emptied
Rains are endless, the tide is strong
They say it won't be long

Darkness comes to chase the day
Tattered sails and flags sway
Howling winds sing a lullaby
With colors hoisted high

Twisted paths—who holds the key?
Heave, ho, 'way we go,
Slaves and thieves, all men are freed
Heave, ho, 'way we go.

Star-touched skin, blood of gold
As it 'twas foretold
Chaos reigns in the realm of Gods
But we will beat the odds!

Twisted paths—who holds the key?
Heave, ho, 'way we go,
Slaves and thieves, all men are freed
Heave, ho, 'way we go."

Laena waited for Zareen to say something—anything. Instead, he stared at her with a look she couldn't quite place.

Her cheeks reddened. "Well?"

"Are you certain it's blood and not seawater that runs through your veins?"

A distant shout sent them both scrambling to their feet. Laena narrowed her eyes to see the faint silhouette of a rowboat, its inhabitant frantically waving his arms.

Zareen folded his and scowled. "Told you it'd be him."

"Please behave."

"I will if he does."

"That's an order, Zareen," Laena snapped. Though she wanted nothing more than to disappear beneath the depths of the waves, she took a step forward, positioning herself between the men she needed to keep from killing one another. Hotah may outmatch her in strength, and Zareen in his passion, but she was still Captain in these parts.

She'd make certain they wouldn't forget.

A Wayward Storm

R. L. Davennor

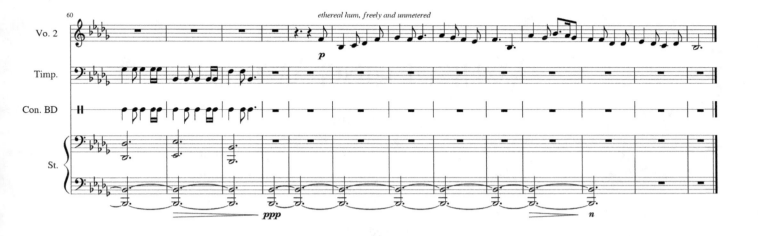

Whispering Wind

Scored for:

Voice
Oboe
Guitar

Bass Drum
String Orchestra

Composed July 2019

Whispering Wind became as emotional as it was originally intended to be an experiment in harmony. As a composer who's used to sticking with traditional and folk-inspired chord progressions, including a secondary dominant that sounds natural to the ear isn't as easy as you might think. With the creation of the lyrics also came the urge to allow the oboe to sing the melody in not just one, but two octaves of its range.

There existed a powerful image in my head. A female bard is strumming aimlessly yet deliberately in the corner of a crowded party sending a hidden message to Rebecca, whom she knows has just married a man she doesn't love. The line 'close your eyes child, don't you cry' is meant to tell her she's not alone.

Listen here:
https://soundcloud.com/rldavennor/whispering-wind

Excerpt from *Bloodlust*, Chapter V. Darkness Falls

Rebecca couldn't yet speak. Instead she buried her fingers into the fabric, glad for the coarseness of the material even though her skin itched. She allowed Naomi to part the curtain and lead the way back into the group, all but collapsing onto a bench lined with pillows and a layer of blankets.

"Rest here until Eleanor arrives."

The chatter died down and the music grew louder. One by one, the shifters joined in to hum a longing melody, allowing the guitar to pluck out a rhythm underneath. Rebecca turned to watch the scene unfold. Their tune was almost beautiful enough to put her to sleep.

Almost.

"The whispering wind floats through the trees
Winter will come and then all will freeze.
A time gone by, a blood-red sky
Close your eyes, child, don't you cry.

Close your eyes, child, don't you cry."

Eventually the shifters returned to their tasks, and as the the song died, the atmosphere in the room returned to normal. The cheerful banter and occasional laughter were a welcome distraction to the maddening silence resonating through Rebecca's skull. Naomi's fingers working out the tangles of her curls offered yet another layer of peace, but it still wasn't nearly enough for Rebecca to sleep.

"Forgive my ignorance," Rebecca whispered, uncertain if Naomi would even hear her. "If you're enslaved, yet a shifter… why don't you just leave?" The secret haven offered anything she could ever want, but even after less than an hour, Rebecca could not shake the feeling of it being… superficial.

Naomi released a breath. "You're not the only one unwilling to leave the ones you love behind."

For the first time, Rebecca closed her eyes. She more than understood.

WHISPERING WIND

R. L. DAVENNOR

Close your eyes child, don't you cry

Winter Waltz

Scored for:

Piano
Celesta
Glockenspiel

Cymbal
Choir
String Orchestra

Composed March 2019

A snowy night in March, as I was listening to ice crystals rain down on my roof, *Winter Waltz* was born. The piano melody came first, and ended up being the centerpiece for the entire piece. I chose to feature piano, cello, and violin as a nod to the traditional arrangement of the piano trio, with everything else added for effect—especially the glockenspiel and celesta. Though the piece is written in 3/4 time, it isn't very waltz-like. The name stuck regardless because the image of a wintery midnight dance wouldn't leave my head.

Listen here:
https://soundcloud.com/rldavennor/winter-waltz

WINTER WALTZ

R. L. DAVENNOR

218

COMING SOON

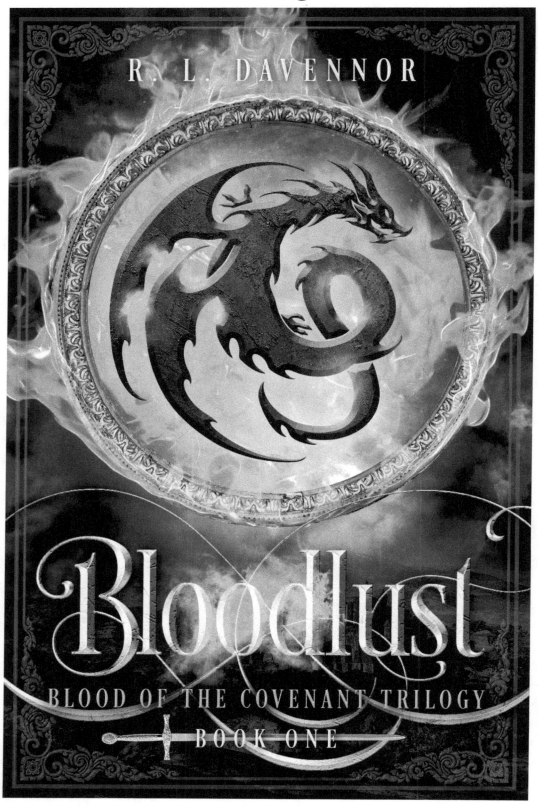

Dragonsblood is more than life.

It's magic.

But Rebecca Marella couldn't care less about hers. She's more concerned with protecting her cousin—even if it means marrying a man she doesn't love.

Even if it means lying through her teeth.

And even if her desperate choices lead her to violence.

Yet for every line she's willing to cross, her enemies are two steps ahead. When tragedy strips Rebecca of everything she's ever known, she's forced to confront the source of her terrifying power.

And mixing with dragons is a dangerous game.

Saving those she loves will mean blood on her hands—but each drop spilled only fuels the darkness within her. The more it feeds, the more ravenous it becomes, and satiating the beast will cost more than Rebecca was ever prepared to give.

She must salvage her humanity or find herself among the very monsters she swore to defeat.

Releasing December 29th, 2020!